PINKY DINKY DOO™

W9-BMX-948

WHERE ARE MY SHOES?

by Jim Jinkins

Level **2** Reader

Special thanks to Katonah Elementary School

Photography by Sandra Kress

Digital coloring and compositing by Alisa Klayman-Grodsky

Published by Creative Edge, 2010, an imprint of Dalmatian Publishing Group, Franklin, Tennessee 37067. No part of this book may be reproduced or copied in any form without written permission from the copyright owner. 1-800-815-8696

"Okay, Tyler!

I'm going to make up a story about

a girl named Pinky Dinky Doo!"

"Hey! That's your name!"

Tyler shouted.

"Exactly!" Pinky Dinky said.

"You just scored a Pinky Dinky Do!"

"All right!" Tyler yelled.

"I'll just shut my eyes,

wiggle my ears,

and crank up
my imagination,"
said Pinky.

"The name of this story is . . ."

WHERE ARE MY SHOES?

A made-up story
by Pinky Dinky Doo

Cool name.

It was a brand-new day in

Great Big City.

Pinky Dinky Doo woke up,

just like always.

Mr. Guinea Pig,

the guinea pig,

gave Pinky Dinky

Doo a big,

sloppy good-

morning kiss.

Pinky jumped out of bed.
She went to the bathroom
and washed her . . .

A Pet guinea pig, Mr. Guinea Pig

B Monster truck,
the Pinky Dinky Dozer

C Face

That's easy!

It's C !
Pinky Dinky Doo
washed her face,
of course!

Downstairs, Pinky ate
a great big bowl of
Frosted Brainiac Flakes.
Then she ran upstairs
to finish getting ready.
But to her surprise,
she couldn't find her shoes!!

Pinky Dinky Doo
looked under
her bed.
No shoes.

Pinky did some
deep-closet diving.

No
shoes!

She even looked in the potty, just in case Tyler had put them there.

No such luck.

This is definitely a Pinky Dinky Don't!

BEEP!

BEEP!

BEEP!

"Oh no!" Pinky said.

"There's the school bus!"

Pinky Dinky didn't know what to do!

"I can't go barefoot," she said.

Pinky Dinky ran from room to room looking for ideas. She put two comfy chairs on her feet. But they were not comfy.

She tried two canoes. But she couldn't find the paddles.

Pinky even put on a pair of clocks. But she was running out of time.

Get it?

"Pinky!"

Mommy Doo shouted.

"Bus! Leave! School! Now!!!"

Pinky was getting exasperated!

X-AS-PER-AY-TED.
It means she was upset.

Book of BIG Words

P.D.D.

Don't forget your lunch!

Pinky Dinky Doo zoomed

to the kitchen.

She grabbed her

double baloney sandwich and

DING!

out of the clear blue sky,

Pinky got an idea!

She opened the sandwich and pulled
out the two pieces of baloney.

Then she wrapped them
around her feet and used
string beans to hold
them in place.

And off Pinky went.

Mommy Doo sighed. "Did my daughter just get on the bus wearing baloney for shoes?"

At school, Pinky Dinky Doo saw
her best friend, Nicholas Biscuit.

Pinky

She told him about
her missing shoes.
"I don't believe it,"
Nicholas shouted.

"Look!"
His feet were
smashed into
two meat loaves.

Meat
loafers

Ketchup
socks

RING!

Just then the bell rang.
It was time for class!

"Come on, Nicholas," Pinky said.
Pinky Dinky Doo and Nicholas
snuck into class.
They hoped no one would see
their crazy shoes.

Their teacher, Ms. Maganza,
was telling the class a true story.
A funny thing happened that day.

"I couldn't find my shoes," she said.
"So I had to wear two roasted chickens!"
Luckily, she had a third chicken
she could use as a purse.
It matched her shoes perfectly.

Instantly, the class was buzzing.
All the kids said they couldn't find
their shoes, either.

Abby B. had wrapped
spaghetti around her feet
to make ballet slippers.

Meatball tutu

Bobby Boom had on
feet-filled doughnuts.

Daffinee Toilette was
wearing melons.

This is so icky!

19

Everybody was talking and laughing and showing off their food shoes. Then Ms. Maganza turned on the TV.

"Attention, all teachers and students! This is Principal Dipthong."

"Due to a mix-up in our school kitchen, today's lunch will be . . .

Slipper Salad

Barbecued Cowboy Boots

And for dessert . . .

Frozen Flip-Flops."

"Gross!"

Daffinee squealed.

"Whoever heard of shoes for lunch?"

"What are we going to do for food?" Bobby moaned.

Pinky Dinky decided to Think Big!

"Stand back!" Nicholas shouted.

Everybody made room

for Pinky to use her brain.

Normally, it was an

everyday, kid-sized brain . . .

until she started to think big!

She thought and thought and thought!

And as she thought,

her brain got bigger and bigger

until her head filled the room.

And then it happened . . .

If you get any brain juice on my dress, I'm telling.

I hope Pinky Dinky Doo comes up with something quick before we get squished!

Pinky had a big idea.

"She's gonna blow!" Nicholas shouted.
The pressure from
all that thinking
shot out of Pinky's ears.
She flew around
the room like a
balloon losing air.

"Hey! I know what we can do!" Pinky said. "Why don't we . . .

A Sit in the corner and drool like baboons?

B Cry like babies with gas?

C Eat our food shoes and wear our shoe food?"

Pinky answered her own question. "It's **C**, of course," she said. "Come on, let's eat our shoes!"

Everyone cheered Pinky's good idea.

Then they all trooped down
to the cafeteria.
Pinky led the way.
First, all the kids
sorted through
the cafeteria dishes
to match up the
pairs of shoes.

Can you help everyone find their missing shoes?

Then they put their food shoes
on the table.

It was a feast of meat loaf,

melon, doughnuts, chicken,

spaghetti, and baloney.

They ate and ate and ate and ate.

It was the best school lunch ever.

"And that's *exactly* what happened.

Sort of," Pinky said to Tyler.

"The end."

Tyler looked worried.

Pinky knew what he was thinking.

"P.S. And since this was a made-up

story, you don't have to worry

about dirty food or germs or

STINKY FEET!" Pinky added.

Tyler was relieved.

"I loved that story!" Tyler yelled.

"Thanks, Tyler," said Pinky.

"Which part did you like best?"

"Uh . . . um . . . I forgot," said Tyler.

"Well," asked Pinky, "did you like
  the girl named Pinky Dinky Stinky?"

"No!" Tyler shouted.

"Her name is Pinky Dinky *Doo*!"

"How about when Pinky got a big, sloppy kiss from Mr. Guinea Pig, the musk ox?" Pinky asked.

"No!" Tyler said.

"Mr. Guinea Pig is a guinea pig!" Mr. Guinea Pig made a funny face.

"Did you like it when Pinky couldn't find her brain?" Pinky asked.

"No!" Tyler shouted. "It was her shoes! She couldn't find her shoes!"

"Wow, Tyler, you remembered
my story really well!" Pinky said.
"Pinky," Tyler asked, "do you think
I'll ever be able to make up stories
as good as yours?"
"Sure!" Pinky said.

"I bet *you* can make up a story, too!"